STEPS TO READING

Dear Parent:

Congratulations! Your child is taking the first steps on an exciting journey. **The destination? Independent reading!**

STEPS TO READING will help your child get there. The programme offers three steps to reading success. Each step includes fun stories and colourful art, and the result is a complete literacy programme with something for every child.

Learning to Read, Step by Step!

(1) **Start to Read   Nursery – Preschool**
• **big type and easy words** • **rhyme and rhythm** • **picture clues**
For children who know the alphabet and are eager to begin reading.

(2) **Let's read together   Preschool – Year 1**
• **basic vocabulary** • **short sentences** • **simple stories**
For children who recognise familiar words and sound out new words with help.

(3) **I can read by myself   Years 1-3**
• **engaging characters** • **easy-to-follow plots** • **popular topics**
For children who are ready to read on their own.

STEPS TO READING is designed to give every child a successful reading experience. The year levels are only guides. Children can progress through the steps at their own speed, developing confidence in their reading, no matter what their year.

*Remember, a lifetime love of reading
starts with a single step!*

By Isabel Gaines
Illustrated by Orlando de la Paz and The Thompson Bros.

This edition published by Parragon in 2011

Parragon
Queen Street House
4 Queen Street
Bath BA1 1HE, UK

ISBN 978-1-4454-2115-5

Printed in Malaysia

Ðisnep

Winnie the Pooh

Pooh's Graduation

PaRRagon

Bath • New York • Singapore • Hong Kong • Cologne • Delhi
Melbourne • Amsterdam • Johannesburg • Auckland • Shenzhen

One morning,
Winnie the Pooh
heard a happy sound.

"Yippee!
I graduated
from first grade,"
said Christopher Robin.

He showed off
his award medal.

"What does
grad-u-a-ted mean?"
asked Pooh.

"It means I finished first grade," said Christopher Robin.

"An award is a prize
for being the best
at something."

"Being the best
sounds hard,"
said Eeyore.

"Let's have our own graduation party," said Christopher Robin.

Christopher Robin
made . . .

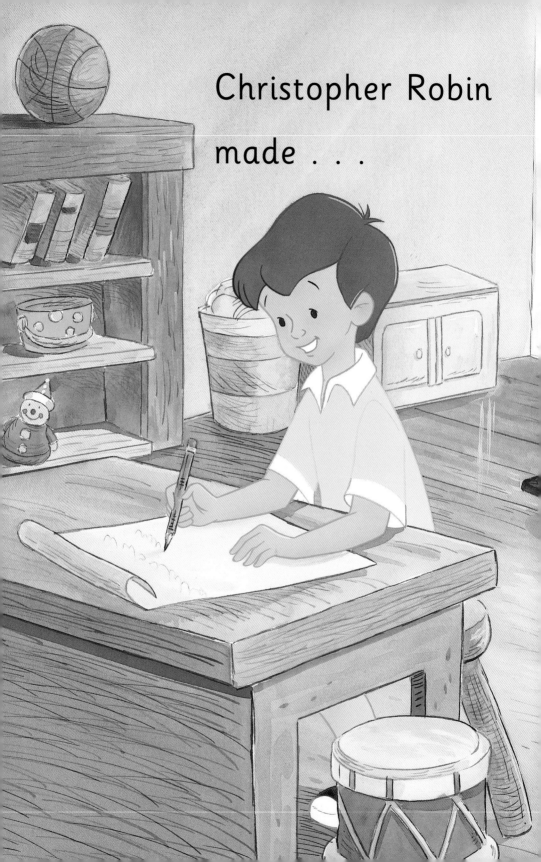

. . . a graduation cap,

a diploma

and an award

for everyone.

Owl practised
giving the
best speech.
Pooh listened.

Kanga tried baking
the best cookies.
Pooh tasted the dough.

Roo finger-painted

lots of pictures.

Pooh picked

the best one.

Pooh helped
Rabbit find
the best carrot.

Pooh helped Piglet
find the best spot
to fly his kite.

Pooh watched
Tigger bounce.

He helped Eeyore

play Pooh Sticks.

Pooh was sleepy
from helping everyone.
"I will take a little nap,"
he said.

Pooh woke up.

He ran out.
He was late
for the party!

Christopher Robin
was handing out
the awards.

"Owl wins the award for Best Speaker!"

"Thank you

so much!"

said Owl.

Kanga won
the award for
Best Cookie Maker.

Roo won

Best Finger-Painter.

Rabbit won

Best Gardener.

Piglet won

Best Kite Flier.

Tigger won
Best Bouncer.

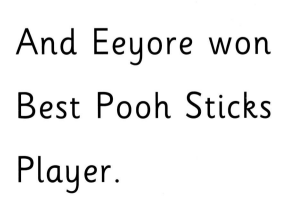

And Eeyore won
Best Pooh Sticks
Player.

Pooh was happy
for his friends.
But he could not think
of anything he did best.

"Pooh wins the award
for being the Best Friend
in the Hundred-Acre Wood!"
said Christopher Robin.

"Me?" said Pooh.
"I did not think I was
best at anything."

"Silly old bear,"
said Christopher Robin.
"You are a best friend."

"Happy graduation!"
said Christopher Robin.

Now turn
over for the
next story...

Adapted by Isabel Gaines
Illustrated by Mark Marderosian and Fred Marvin

Dᴉsney
Winnie the Pooh

I love you Mama

Bath · New York · Singapore · Hong Kong · Cologne · Delhi
Melbourne · Amsterdam · Johannesburg · Auckland · Shenzhen

One day,
Tigger and Roo
were out bouncing.

They bounced up to
Christopher Robin.

"Hello!" said Tigger
and Roo.

"Hi!" said
Christopher Robin.

"Tomorrow is
Mother's Day,"
said Christopher Robin.

"Yay!" said Roo.
"I want to give Mama
a surprise."

"Tiggers love surprises!"
said Tigger.
"So do mothers!"
said Roo.

Christopher Robin
had an idea.
"We can have
a surprise party,"
he said.

All the friends
got together.
They planned
the party.

The next morning, Roo remembered something. He had forgotten to get Mama a present.

Roo looked for
something to give Mama.
But he only had toys.

Roo heard a knock
at the front door.
He ran out of his room.
It was time
for the party.

Kanga opened the door.
"HAPPY MOTHER'S DAY!"
everyone shouted.

"Thank you!"
Kanga said.

"Sit in your
favourite chair,
Mama!" said Roo.

"Time for presents!"

said Roo.

Eeyore gave Kanga
some droopy flowers.

"Tigger has something,
too," said Roo.

Tigger gave Kanga
a bouncy bunch
of flowers.

"My flowers are not
as nice as Tigger's,"
said Eeyore.
"Your flowers are
pretty, too,"
said Kanga.

Christopher Robin

gave out

homemade muffins.

Rabbit gave Kanga
vegetables from
his garden.

Piglet gave Kanga
a big cake.

Pooh gave her
a pot of honey.

"Now Owl will say a poem," said Roo.

"Kanga is a mother
unlike any other.
She cares for us all
even when we fall,"
said Owl.

Kanga clapped.
Owl took a bow.

It was Roo's turn.
But he did not have
a gift for Kanga.
He started to cry.
"I forgot to get you
a present," he said.

"But I already have the best present ever," said Kanga.

"You do?" asked Roo.

"Yes!" said Kanga.

"I have you!"